Johnny on the Spot

by Edward Sorel

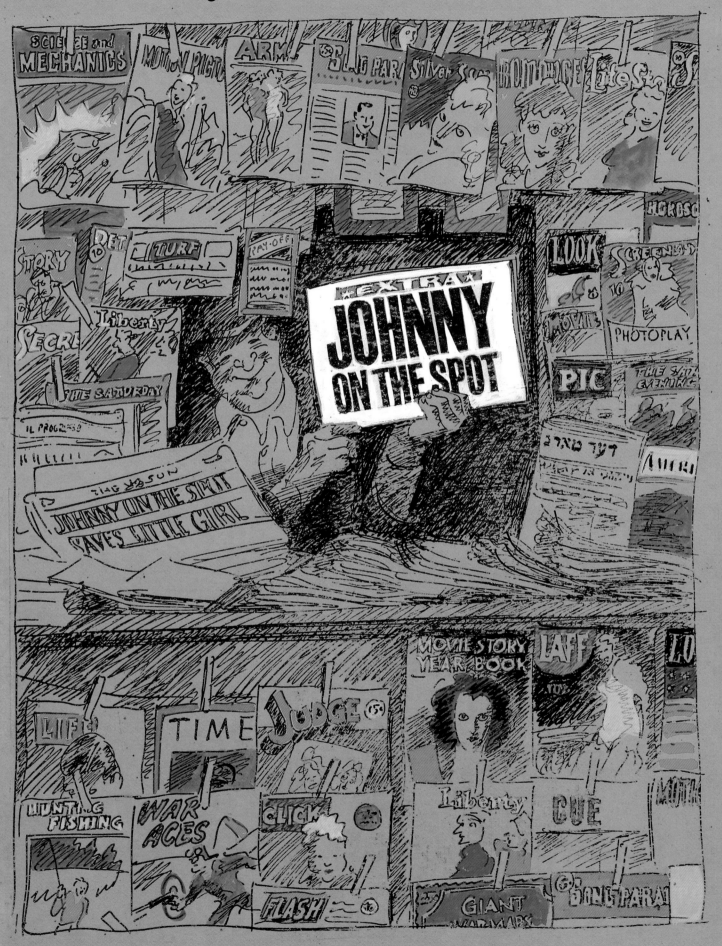

Margaret K. McElderry Books

To Saskia and Sabella

Margaret K. McElderry Books
An imprint of Simon & Schuster Children's Publishing Division
1230 Avenue of the Americas
New York, New York 10020
Copyright © 1998 by Edward Sorel
All rights reserved, including the right of reproduction in whole or in part in any form.
Book design by Edward Sorel and Ann Bobco
The text of this book is set in Century Schoolbook.
The illustrations were rendered in pen and ink and watercolor.
Printed in Hong Kong by South China Printing Co. (1988) Ltd.
First Edition
10 9 8 7 6 5 4 3 2 1
Library of Congress Cataloging-in-Publication Data:
Sorel, Edward, 1929-
Johnny on the spot / Edward Sorel.—1st ed.
p. cm.
Summary: When Johnny's radio begins to broadcast the news from tomorrow,
he begins a series of heroic and lucrative adventures.
ISBN 0-689-81293-0
[1. Radio broadcasting—Fiction.] I. Title.
PZ7.S716Jo 1997
[Fic]—dc20 96-22218 CIP AC

H IDDEN UNDER A TOWERING BRIDGE stood a row of mixed-up build-
ings. No two were alike. Johnny lived in the one on the corner.
In his apartment he always heard the sound of speeding cars
rushing across the bridge to faraway places. Someday, when he grew up, he
too would travel and have exciting adventures, just like the hero of his
favorite radio serial, "Don Winslow of the Navy." Johnny listened to the Don
Winslow program every day. Even though it was summertime and there
was no school, he always ran home when the program was about to begin.

Johnny knew that Don Winslow was not a real person and that the stories about his adventures were just make-believe, but that didn't keep him from enjoying them. For weeks Johnny had been listening to a story about a master criminal, known as The Scorpion, who had invented a death ray with which he hoped to conquer the world. And he would, if Don Winslow didn't stop him.

Johnny had to sit very close to his old Zenith radio because the sound had gotten weak lately.

One day, Don Winslow had fallen into a trap and was fighting three thugs to get free when the radio suddenly went dead. It was an awful time for the radio to conk out, but Johnny had been expecting it. The sound had been getting fainter and fainter, while the static kept getting noisier. In the past he had sometimes been able to make the radio perform by slapping the side of the cabinet that held it. But not this time. The only sound was a low, steady hum. The old radio was completely, absolutely, and positively dead.

That evening, when his parents came home from work, Johnny wasted no time in telling them about the radio. "You mean I won't have to listen to static anymore?" said his father as he walked into the kitchen. Johnny followed him and asked if they couldn't buy a new radio. "Look, Johnny," his father said as he slumped in a chair, "we still owe the money we borrowed from Uncle Timothy when you took sick. Until we pay him back, we can't spend money on anything except food and rent."

Johnny almost gave up hope, but the next day he remembered Mr. Zaga, the mysterious man who lived in an apartment in the basement. Mr. Zaga was said to be an inventor, and he might be willing to fix the radio just as a favor. Johnny disconnected it from the cabinet and carried it down to Mr. Zaga's apartment. But when the door opened, Johnny could see that it wasn't an apartment at all. It was a laboratory with lots of weird, complicated machinery.

After Johnny explained why he had come, Mr. Zaga placed the radio on a long table and studied it. "I don't know much about sound transmission," he admitted. "My specialty is time travel, but my electrostatic magnetron

isn't powerful enough to transport me into the future. So far I've only been able to travel one day ahead." It suddenly occurred to Johnny that Mr. Zaga might be crazy, but that didn't mean he couldn't fix the radio.

"Maybe all your radio needs," suggested Mr. Zaga, "is a small charge of electrostatic magnetism." He gave Johnny a pair of goggles and put a pair over his own eyes. Then he placed the radio under the magnetron and pulled the switch. A powerful ray poured from the spooky-looking machine into the radio, turning its tubes bright red. They were beginning to turn purple when Mr. Zaga shut the magnetron off. After the radio cooled down, he carried it back to Johnny's apartment and reconnected the wires. "Well, young man," he said, "switch it on."

Johnny turned the knob and let out a shout of joy. *The radio played perfectly!* He heard a news broadcaster giving the weather report: "The city has recovered from yesterday's torrential downpour and is now enjoying bright sunshine." Mr. Zaga was puzzled. It was storming outside.

Then the sports news came on. Johnny was eager to hear how the Giants had done against the Phillies. But instead he heard about a game between the Giants and the Dodgers. "That's crazy," said Johnny. "The Giants don't play the Dodgers until tomorrow!"

Mr. Zaga and Johnny stared at each other, baffled. Then suddenly Mr. Zaga jumped in the air, shouting, "I've done it! I've done it!" Johnny looked more puzzled than ever. "Don't you see?" screamed Mr. Zaga. "I've sent your radio into the future! *It's a day ahead!*"

Johnny tried to understand. "You mean my radio thinks it's tomorrow? You mean today is yesterday to my radio?"

"Exactly so," said Mr. Zaga, plopping into the easy chair with a big smile on his face.

Suddenly a radio voice cut into the music that was playing. "We interrupt this program to bring you an important news bulletin. The East Side Savings Bank on Grand Street was robbed this afternoon by three armed men. Bank officials estimate that the thieves made off with over forty thousand dollars."

"That bank is only a few blocks from here," Mr. Zaga said.

"I know," Johnny answered. "We should go right over and warn them that they're going to be robbed tomorrow."

"No, no," said Mr. Zaga. "We must never do anything that interferes with the future. And another thing—as long as your parents think the radio is dead, don't tell them what we've done. I need time to think about all this."

Johnny saw no harm in that, but that night as he tried to fall asleep, he kept thinking about the bank robbery that was going to take place tomorrow, just a few blocks away.

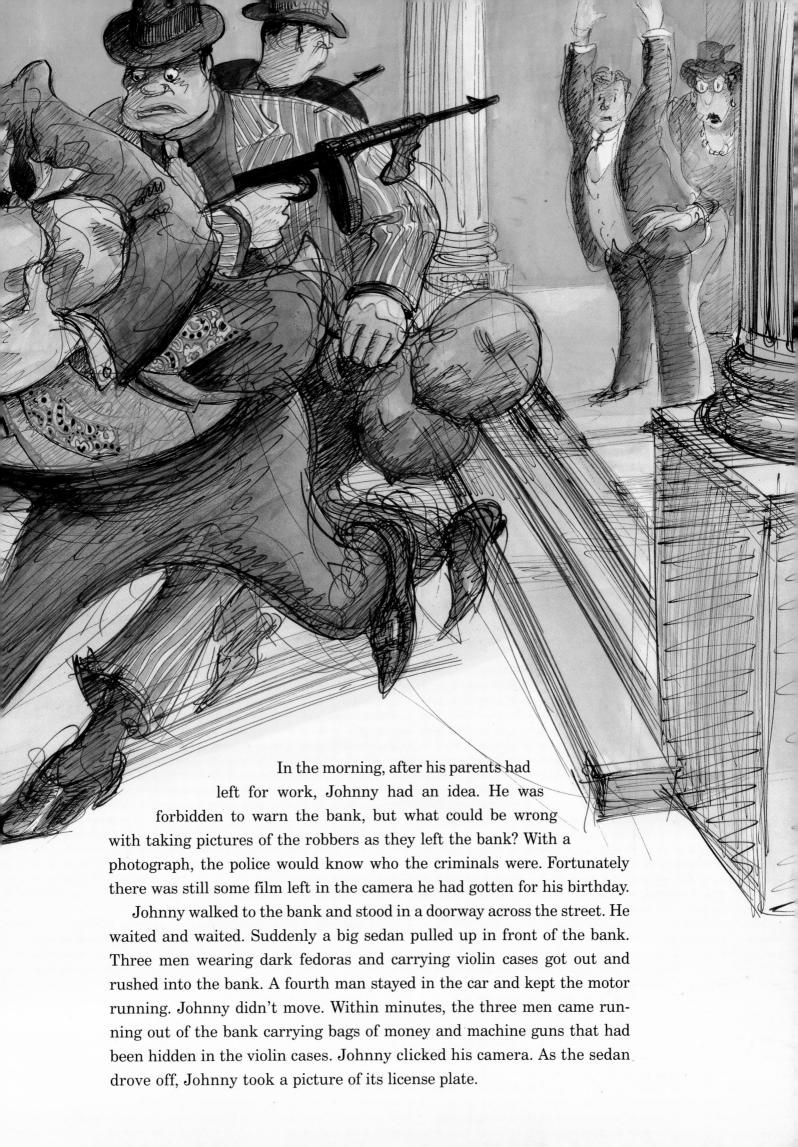

In the morning, after his parents had
left for work, Johnny had an idea. He was
forbidden to warn the bank, but what could be wrong
with taking pictures of the robbers as they left the bank? With a
photograph, the police would know who the criminals were. Fortunately
there was still some film left in the camera he had gotten for his birthday.

Johnny walked to the bank and stood in a doorway across the street. He
waited and waited. Suddenly a big sedan pulled up in front of the bank.
Three men wearing dark fedoras and carrying violin cases got out and
rushed into the bank. A fourth man stayed in the car and kept the motor
running. Johnny didn't move. Within minutes, the three men came running out of the bank carrying bags of money and machine guns that had
been hidden in the violin cases. Johnny clicked his camera. As the sedan
drove off, Johnny took a picture of its license plate.

Just then, a man ran out of the bank straight to Johnny. "Listen, kid," he said excitedly. "If those pictures you just took come out, I know who'll pay big bucks for them." Before Johnny could ask any questions, the man hailed a taxi and pushed Johnny inside. "The *Mirror* building, and step on it!" he told the driver.

The next thing Johnny knew, he and the man were in the editor's office at *The Mirror,* a daily newspaper, waiting for the film to be developed. When the pictures finally came, the editor took one look at them and shouted, "Stop the presses! We've got a new photo for the front page!"

The editor decided to run a story on the young photographer as well as the photograph. In the story Johnny was referred to as "Johnny-on-the-spot." A reporter drove him home, and Johnny's mother and father sat speechless as he told them about everything that had happened that day. "And now for the best part," he said, pulling five crisp bills out of his pocket. "They paid me *fifty dollars!*"

Johnny wanted his father to take the money and pay back Uncle Timothy, but his father said, "No, no. It's your money—you earned it. Maybe you ought to buy yourself a new radio."

Of course, the last thing Johnny wanted now was a new radio. In the morning, as soon as his parents left for work, he switched on the old one. It had become something magical. Now he was able to listen to the news and know what was going to happen tomorrow—to know something that no one else knew. As he sprawled in the easy chair admiring his crisp ten-dollar bills, he heard the broadcaster reporting news of a fire in an apartment house on Polk Street. Polk Street was only three blocks from his own house. What should he do?

He decided to go downstairs and talk to Mr. Zaga. Perhaps this time Mr. Zaga would allow him to warn people about what was going to happen to them. But as soon as Johnny entered the laboratory, he saw that Mr. Zaga was upset. "I don't understand it," he wailed. "I've tried to make these radios do what yours does, but not one of them has traveled into the future." The unhappy inventor slumped into a chair, completely defeated. Johnny could see this wasn't a good time to talk to him.

He was going to have to reach this decision by himself.

The next morning Johnny hurried to Polk Street. He knew that if he tried to warn the people in the building, they would just think he was loony. In an empty lot across from the building that was going to burn, Johnny waited. Nearby a noisy steam shovel was digging up the ground. The moment Johnny spied smoke coming out of a third-floor window, he ran to a fire alarm box and called in the alarm. Running back to the building, he saw a little girl at an open window, crying for help.

Thinking fast, Johnny ran to the operator of the steam shovel. Pointing to the trapped child, Johnny asked him if he thought he could raise him high enough in the shovel to reach her. "I'll try," the man said. The operator drove close to the burning building. As soon as he climbed into the bucket, Johnny felt himself hoisted higher and higher. The little girl, understanding that someone was trying to save her, held out her arms. Johnny grabbed her and pulled her into the bucket.

Once she realized she was safe, the little girl stopped crying, but she still clung to Johnny. He could hear fire engines clanging closer. By the time the bucket touched the ground, the firemen had their hoses going, and news photographers were snapping pictures right and left. They asked Johnny his name and where he lived. Then a policeman took the little girl from his arms, patted his back, said, "Good job, kid!" and sent him home in a police car. His parents weren't there, and he was so tired he fell onto his bed, sound asleep.

The next day was Saturday. Johnny's parents slept late on Saturdays, but this time they were awakened early by a neighbor who had read about Johnny in the morning paper. Soon other friends and relatives showed up. Their loud talking finally woke Johnny. He couldn't imagine what was going on until Uncle Timothy held up a copy of *The Mirror*. The headline read, Johnny-on-the-Spot Saves Tot. Then Johnny understood why they were all there. They were proud of him.

For the rest of that weekend, everyone kept telling Johnny how brave he was. On Monday, though, he found himself alone again. Around noon, Mr. Zaga appeared. He got right to the point. "Are you aware that there's a radio station that gives racing results? You and I now have the power to know ahead of time which horse will win each race. If we bet on the winner, we will quickly become very, very rich."

Johnny looked troubled. "I couldn't," he said. "I promised my mother I'd never gamble." Mr. Zaga became irritated. "But it's not gambling," he exploded. "We *know* which horse will win."

The following day, Johnny and Mr. Zaga arrived at the racetrack with
the names of all the horses that would win that day. Johnny had his fifty
dollars in his pocket, and Mr. Zaga had all the money he owned. They were
early, so they had time to watch the horses as they paraded in a circle
before the race began. Johnny thought they were the most beautiful horses
he had ever seen. The horse they were going to bet on in the first race was
called Sleepytime Gal, and she really did look tired. Johnny wondered if he
should bet his whole fifty dollars on her, but Mr. Zaga said, "Stop worrying.
She'll wake up when the race begins."

And there really was nothing to worry about. Sleepytime Gal won, just as the radio had said she would. So did the other horses Johnny and Mr. Zaga bet on in the second, third, and fourth races. But then Johnny ran into a problem he hadn't foreseen. He had won so much money, he had no place to put it. His pockets were full, and there were still three more races.

"Next time we'll bring a suitcase," Mr. Zaga sighed. "But I think we can bet on one more race today. If your winnings won't fit into your pockets, just stuff them inside your knickers."

After betting on a horse named Jitterbug, Mr. Zaga wanted to stay at the cashier's window, but Johnny insisted they watch the race, even

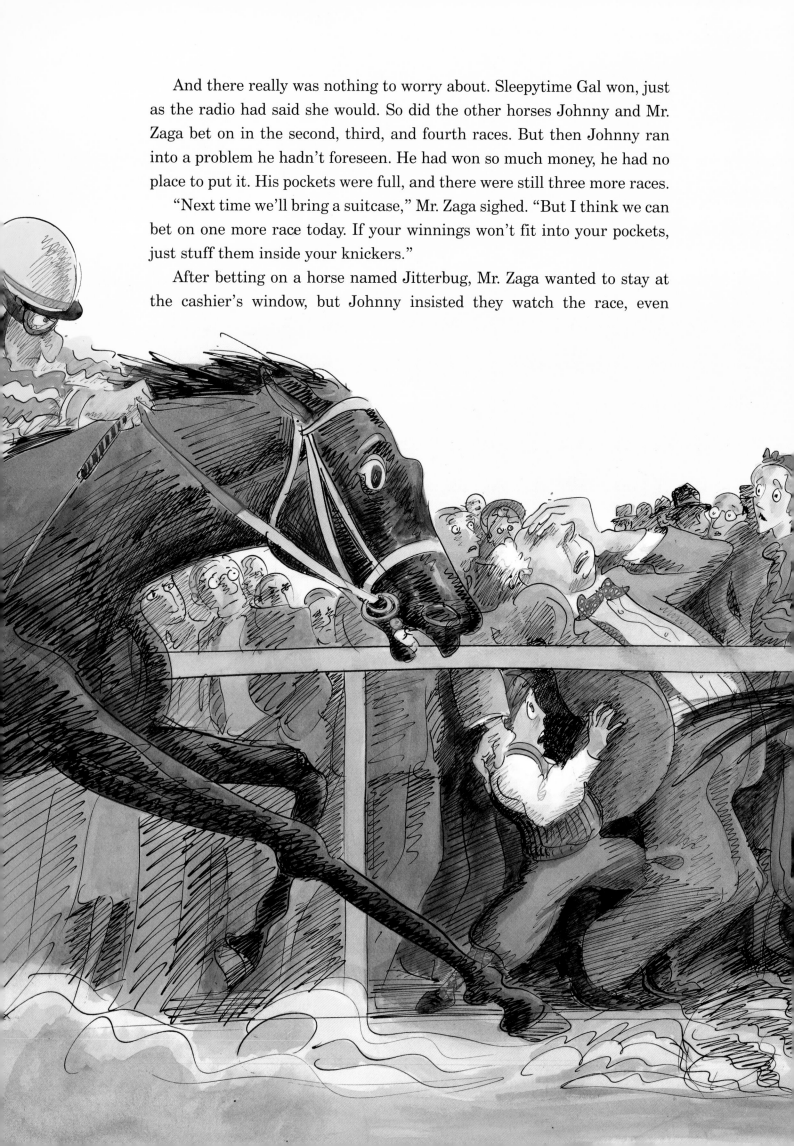

though they knew how it would end. As the horses thundered into the last stretch, Johnny and Mr. Zaga were horrified to see Jitterbug running second. When another horse crossed the finish line ahead of Jitterbug, Mr. Zaga clutched his head and would have passed out if he hadn't had Johnny to lean on.

If only they had left after the fourth race, Johnny kept thinking. But just as he felt tears in his eyes, a voice came over the loudspeaker. The winning horse was disqualified for interfering with another horse. Jitterbug was declared the official winner.

Johnny and Mr. Zaga took a taxi home. Once in their building, Mr. Zaga followed Johnny upstairs so that he could listen to the names of tomorrow's winners. Johnny found it difficult to walk up the stairs because his knickers were stuffed with dollar bills. When he opened the door, he was surprised to find his parents already home, and even more surprised to hear music coming out of a radio. Johnny and Mr. Zaga stared pop-eyed at the spot where the old Zenith had been. In its place was a shiny, brand new Philco. Where had it come from?

"It's a present for you from Uncle Timothy," explained Johnny's father.

"B-b-but what did you do with the old radio?" Johnny asked, unable to hide his panic.

"I gave it to the junkman," said his father.

Just then Johnny's mother noticed some dollar bills sticking out of her son's knickers. It was time for Johnny to tell the whole story about the radio. Mr. Zaga added a few details—such as that going to the racetrack had been entirely his idea. At the end, Johnny emptied his pockets and knickers of the money. It made quite a pile.

In all the excitement everyone lost track of time. Johnny's mother asked Mr. Zaga to stay for dinner, and over servings of corned beef and cabbage, he told them about his plans for the future. He had decided to forget about inventing a time machine. "Instead, I'm going to work on a radio that will also show pictures," he said. "I think I'll call it 'radiovision.'"

There was a long silence. Johnny could tell that his parents thought Mr. Zaga was crazy. Johnny, on the other hand, believed that anything was possible—even a radio that showed pictures. And he hoped he'd be on-the-spot when it happened.